To ....

For being good.

MERRY CHRISTMAS!

From Santa

D1311808

Santa is coming to Kansas City

Written by Steve Smallman
Illustrated by Robert Dunn and Alan Brown
Designed by Sarah Allen

Copyright © Hometown World Ltd. 2013

Sourcebooks and the colophon are registered trademarks of Sourcebooks, Inc.
All rights reserved. No part of this book may be reproduced in any form or by any electronic or mechanical means including information storage and retrieval systems—except in the case of brief quotations embodied in critical articles or reviews—without permission in writing from its publisher, Sourcebooks, Inc.

The characters and events portrayed in this book are fictitious or are used fictitiously. Any similarity to real persons, living or dead, is purely coincidental and not intended by the author.

Published by Sourcebooks Jabberwocky, an imprint of Sourcebooks, Inc.
P.O. Box 4410, Naperville, Illinois 60567-4410
(630) 961-3900
Fax: (630) 961-2168
www.jabberwockykids.com

Library of Congress Cataloging-in-Publication data is on file with the publisher.

Source of Production: Leo Paper Products, Guangdong Province, China
Date of Production: April 2014
Run Number: HTW_PO170314
Printed and bound in China
LEO 10 9 8 7 6 5 4 3 2

Santa is coming to Kansas City

Written by Steve Smallman
Illustrated by Robert Dunn and Alan Brown

sourcebooks
jabberwocky

"Well?"

boomed Santa. "Have all the children from **Kansas City** been good this year?"

"Well...uh...mostly," answered the little old elf, as he bustled across the busy workshop to Santa's desk.

Santa peered down at the elf from behind the tall, teetering piles of letters that the children of Kansas City had sent him.

"Mostly?" asked Santa, looking over the top of his glasses.

"Yes...but they've all been **especially** good in the last few days!" said the elf.

"Jolly good!" chuckled Santa,
"Then we'd better get their presents loaded up!"

Even though the sack of presents was

really, really big

and the elves were **really, really** small,

they seemed to have no trouble loading it onto Santa's sleigh.
Though how they managed to fit such a big sack into one little sleigh
even they didn't know. But somehow they did.

"Splendid!" boomed Santa. "We're ready to go!"

"Er...not quite, Santa," said the little old elf. "One of our reindeer is missing!"

"Missing?

Which reindeer is missing?" asked Santa.

"The youngest one, Santa," said the elf. "It's his first flight tonight. I've called him and called him, but..."

Just then, a young reindeer strolled up, munching on a large carrot.

"where have you been?"

asked Santa.

But the youngest reindeer was crunching so loudly that it was no wonder he hadn't heard the little old elf calling.

"Oh well, never mind," said Santa, giving the reindeer a little wink. He took out his Santa-nav and tapped in the coordinates for Kansas City. **"This will guide us to Kansas City in no time."**

Crunch!
Crunch!
Crunch!

With a flick of the reins and a jerk of the harness, off they went, racing through the sky.

"Ho, ho, ho!"
laughed Santa.

"We'll soon have these presents delivered to K.C.!"

Santa's sleigh flew through the starry night, heading south across the Arctic Ocean. On they flew in the crisp, wintry air, crossing over Canada. In the wink of an eye, the sleigh was flying above the Great Lakes and over Missouri. The youngest reindeer was very excited. He had never been away from the North Pole before.

They were just crossing Smithville Lake
when, suddenly, they ran into a blizzard.
Snowflakes swirled around the sleigh.

They couldn't see a thing!

The youngest reindeer was getting a bit worried,
but Santa didn't seem concerned.

"In two miles..."

said the Santa-nav in a bossy lady's voice,

"...keep left at the next star."

"But, ma'am," Santa blustered, "I can't see any stars in all this snow!"
Soon they were

hopelessly lost!

Ding-dong!
Ding-dong!

Then, through the howling blizzard, the youngest reindeer heard a faint, ringing sound.

Ding-dong!

He looked over at the old reindeer with the red nose. But he had his head down.

(Red nose...I wonder who that could be?)

Ding-dong
Ding-dong!

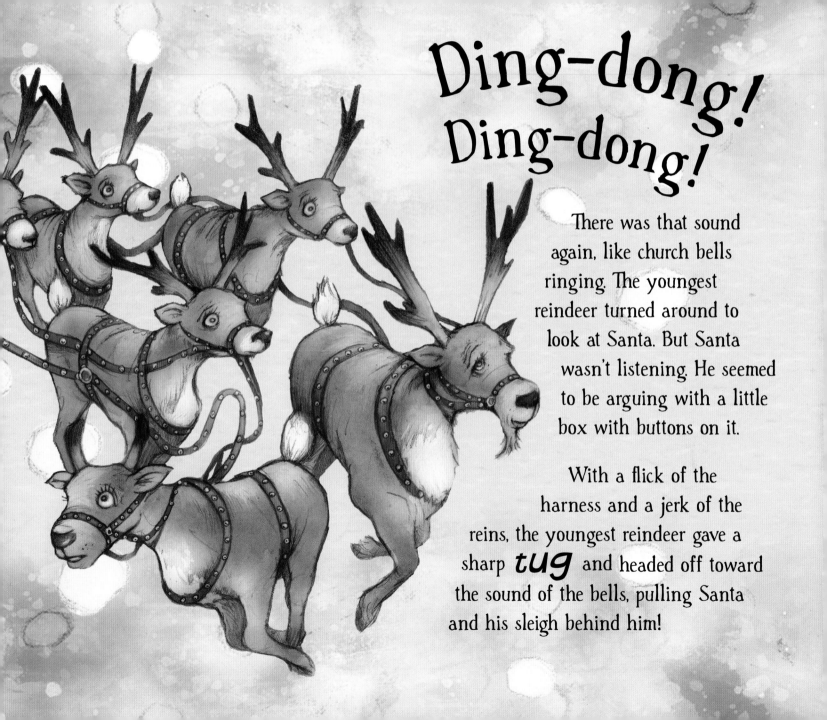

Ding-dong! Ding-dong!

There was that sound again, like church bells ringing. The youngest reindeer turned around to look at Santa. But Santa wasn't listening. He seemed to be arguing with a little box with buttons on it.

With a flick of the harness and a jerk of the reins, the youngest reindeer gave a sharp *tug* and headed off toward the sound of the bells, pulling Santa and his sleigh behind him!

"Whoa!"

cried Santa, pulling his hat straight.
"What's going on?" Then, to his surprise,
he heard the ringing sound.

"Well done, young reindeer!" he shouted cheerfully,
"It must be the Cathedral of the Immaculate
Conception. Don't worry, children, Santa is coming!"

Then, suddenly...

CRUNCH!

The sleigh hit something as it plummeted through the snow clouds. **"You have arrived!"** said the Santa-nav unhelpfully.

Finally, when the fog had lifted, Santa discovered exactly where they were...

...stuck, right at the very top of the Kansas City **Power and Light Building!**

"Everybody, PULL!"

The reindeer *pulled* with all their might until, at last, with a
screeching noise, the sleigh scraped clear of the tower and Santa
steered them safely above Crown Center, over the Plaza, across
Brush Creek, and down into Jacob L. Loose Park.

Luckily, there
was no real
damage done, but
the packages had all
been jumbled up. Santa
quickly sorted out the
presents into order again.

"All right," said Santa. "Thanks
to this young reindeer I know where
we are now. Don't worry, children,

Santa is coming!"

Santa drove his sleigh expertly from rooftop to rooftop all over Kansas City, popping in and out of chimneys as fast as he could go.

(Which was pretty fast for a chubby fellow!)

There were big chimneys in Gladstone, and small chimneys in Prairie Village. He squeezed down thin chimneys in Brookside and plummeted down fat chimneys in Fairway.

The youngest reindeer was amazed at how quickly they went. Santa never seemed to get tired at all! And it looked like the children in Kansas City were going to be very lucky this year! But the youngest reindeer was starting to feel a bit weary and quite hungry too!

In house after house, Santa delved inside his sack for packages of every shape and size.

He piled them under the Christmas trees and carefully filled up the stockings with surprises.

Santa took a little bite out of each cookie,
a tiny sip of milk, wiped his beard, and
popped the carrots into his sack.

In house after house, the good children
of Kansas City had left out a plate of
cookies, a small glass of milk and, a big,
crunchy carrot.

From Strawberry Hill to Blue Hills, from Westwood to Winnwood, from Olathe to Overland Park, and ALL the places in between, Santa and his sleigh visited every house in Kansas City.

Santa delivered presents to Andrew, Anson, Anna, Arabella, Archie, Ashley...the list went on and on! ...Zac, Zara, Zeb, Zoe, Zybil.

(Zybil? That must be a spelling mistake, surely!)

Finally, Santa had delivered the
last present on his long Kansas City list.

"Great moons and stars!" sighed
Santa. "It's past midnight and my sack seems as
heavy as ever! I hope I haven't forgotten anyone."

Santa opened his sack to check...but it was full
of juicy, crunchy carrots!

Santa divided the carrots among all the reindeer.
"Well, done!" he said, patting the youngest reindeer gently on the nose.

But the youngest reindeer didn't hear him...
he was too busy munching!

Then it was time to set off for home. Santa reset his Santa-nav once more
to the North Pole, and soon they were speeding over the Missouri River,
above Holland Park, and out past the Fairfax Bridge.